Disney

Tim Burton's

The Nightmare Before Christmas

Zero's Journey

Book Two

WRITTEN BY
D.J. MILKY

COVER BY
KIYOSHI ARAI

STORYBOARDS AND PENCILS BY
KEI ISHIYAMA

INKS BY
DAVID HUTCHISON

COLORS BY
DAN CONNER

CONTENTS

◇◇◇◇◇◇◇◇◇◇◇◇◇◇◇◇◇◇◇◇◇◇◇◇◇◇◇

ISSUE #5 5

ISSUE #6 25

ISSUE #7 45

ISSUE #8 65

ISSUE #9 85

COVER ART GALLERY 106

CONCEPT ART GALLERY........ 116

PREVIOUSLY ON...

ZERO'S JOURNEY

AFTER ACCIDENTALLY SETTING OFF ONE OF JACK'S HALLOWEEN INVENTIONS, ZERO FOUND HIMSELF WHISKED AWAY TO CHRISTMAS TOWN! EXPLORING THE BUSY VILLAGE, HE MET MANY COLORFUL CHARACTERS – SOME KINDER THAN OTHERS – AND GORGED HIMSELF ON DELICIOUS BAKED TREATS. BUT WHEN HE CHOWED DOWN ON A LIVING GINGERBREAD MAN, ZERO MIGHT HAVE BITTEN OFF MORE THAN HE COULD CHEW.

MEANWHILE, BESIDE HIMSELF WITH WORRY, JACK SENT A RESCUE TEAM OF LOCK, SHOCK AND BARREL THROUGH THE FOREST PORTAL TO BRING ZERO HOME. THE THREE MISCHIEVOUS SCAMPS PROMISED THEY WOULDN'T GET INTO TOO MUCH TROUBLE...

THUD
YIPPEE-YAY!
WE SAY NO!
MERRY CHRISTMAS?
GET OUT OF OUR WAY! WE'RE HERE TO PLAY!
WE BRING TROUBLE!

GUYS, LET'S HUDDLE!
ON THE DOUBLE...
AND LOCK, YOU CHOOSE ANYWHERE.
YOU GO THAT WAY, I'LL GO THERE.
ON THE COUNT OF THREE, IT'S TIME THEY SEE HOW CHRISTMAS TOWN SHOULD REALLY BE!
YEA!
YEA!
YEA!
YAHOOOO!

CANDY'S WHAT I LOVE THE MOST!
NO NEED TO BRAG OR EVEN BOAST!
I'M THE BEST, THE WHOLE WORLD KNOWS ...
...AT TRICK-OR-TREATIN', COAST TO COAST!

WOW...
YUMMM!

HAHAAH!
SLUSH
SLUSH
BUMP
HAHAAH!
THUD

SO NOW IT'S MY TURN TO GRAB A SLEIGH.
THIS HOLIDAY IS FILLED WITH JOY, THEY SAY.
WATCH ME NOW! MOVE OVER OR YOU'LL PAY!
I PUT THE JOY IN JOYRIDE, DOING THINGS MY WAY!

HOP
WHEEEEE!!!

I LOVE THE SMELL OF...
DELICIOUS GRUB!

CHATTER
CHATTER
I EAT SO MUCH THEY ALL CALL ME A TUB!
GROWWWL
BUT TAKE NO HEED 'CAUSE, AY...
THERE'S THE RUB!
25.5
12

A HAPPY MOUTH.
MAKES FOR A ROLY-POLY CHUB!
THE KING OF CANES!
UP THIS STUPID TREE, I CLIMB!
IT'LL BE ALL MINE!

CREAK
CREAK
I'VE GOT IT!
LOCK'S ON TOP THIS TIME!
UH-OH...

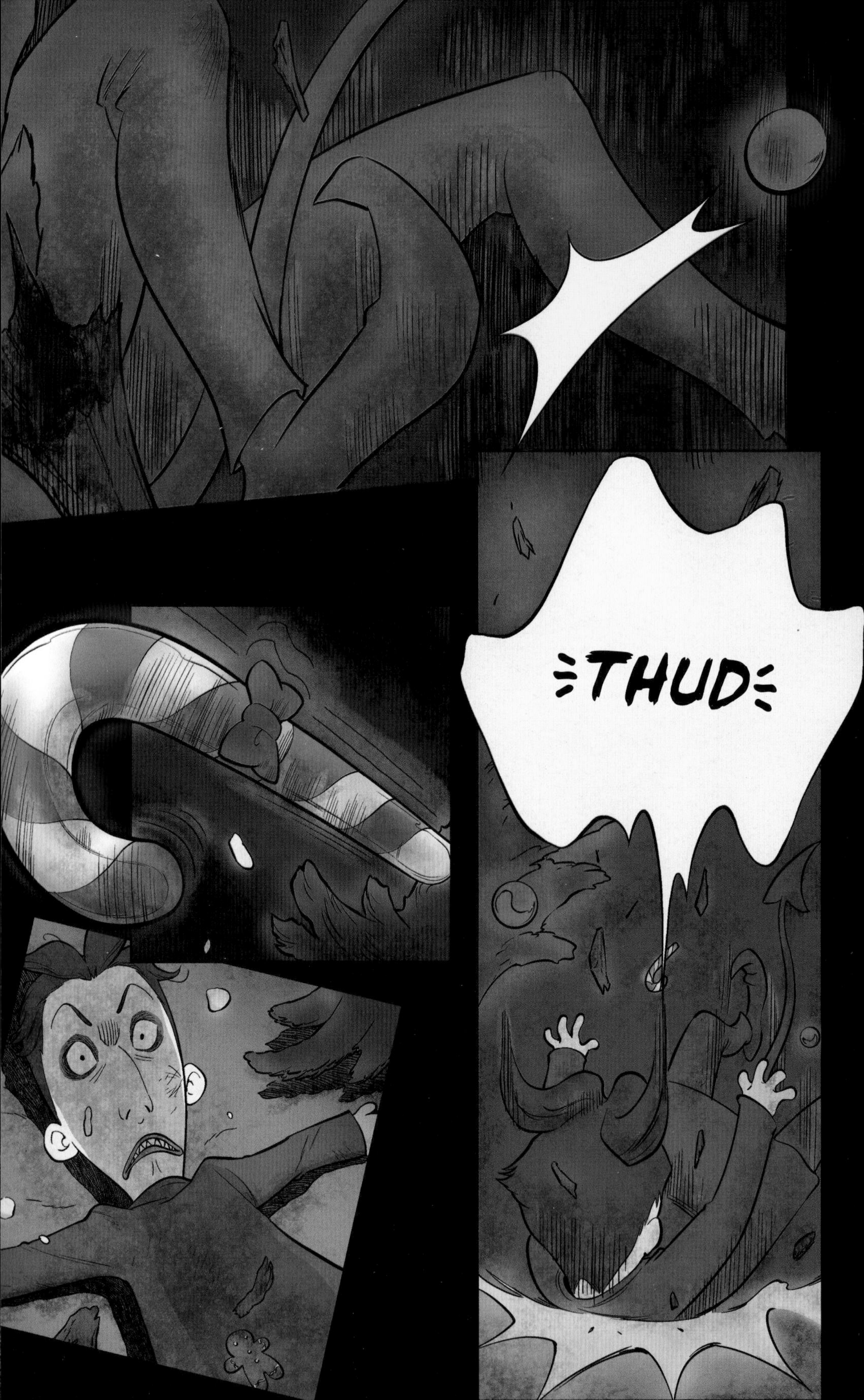
THUD

AHHHH!

SMASH

...

OOOH, NOTHING LIKE THIS CRAZY WINTER BLAST!
SPEED!
I LOVE TO GO SO FAST!
WOOOOOO-HOOOOO!

WAIT, THE BRAKES!
THIS SLEIGH!
IT JUST MIGHT...
AH
AH
AH
AGGGHHH!!

CRASH...

TWITCH
PLEASE GIVE ME ALL THE SCRUMPTIOUS FOOD.

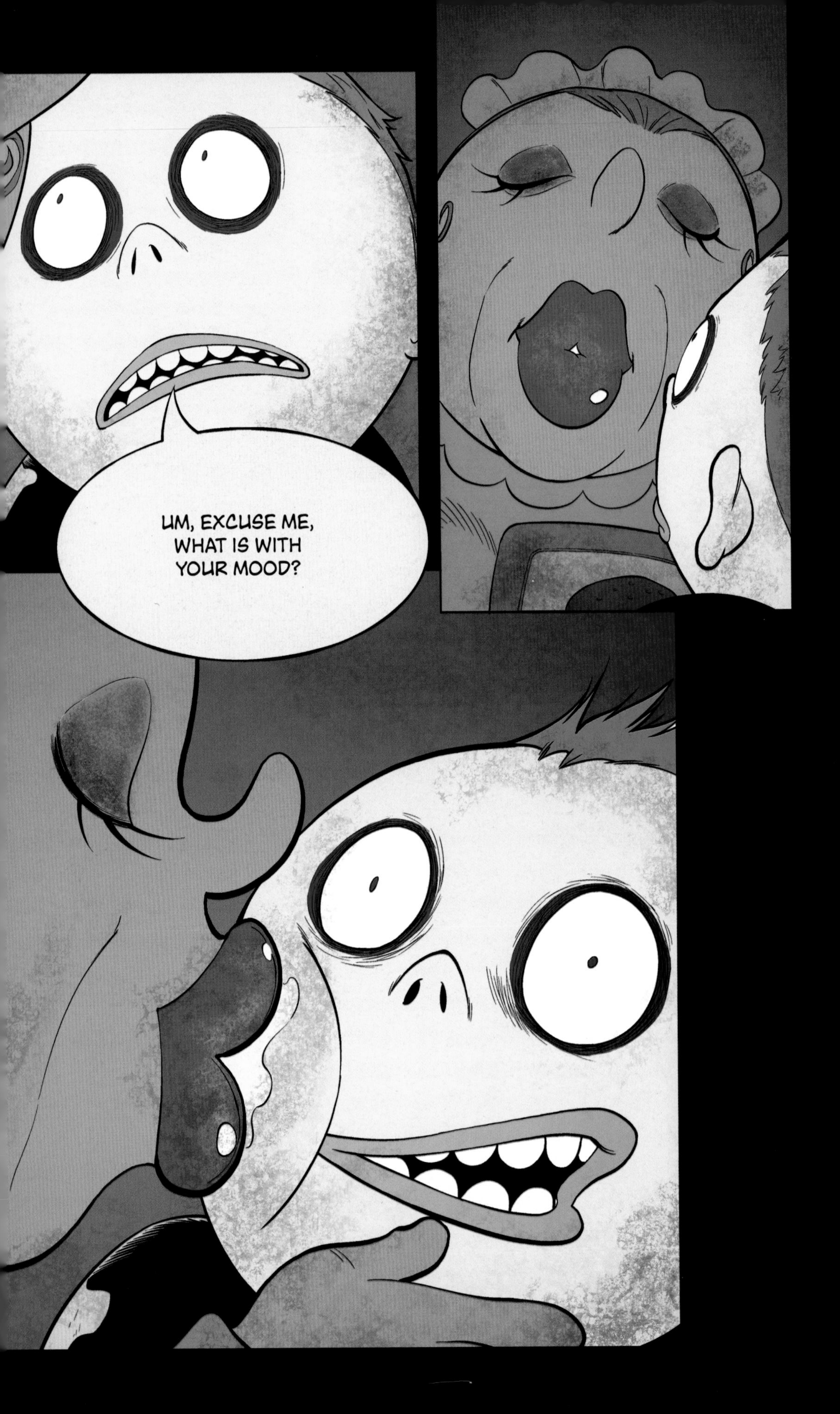
UM, EXCUSE ME,
WHAT IS WITH
YOUR MOOD?

HEY!
WHAT ARE YOU DOING!
THAT'S SO... RUDE!

EEEWWWWWWW!
PANT
PANT

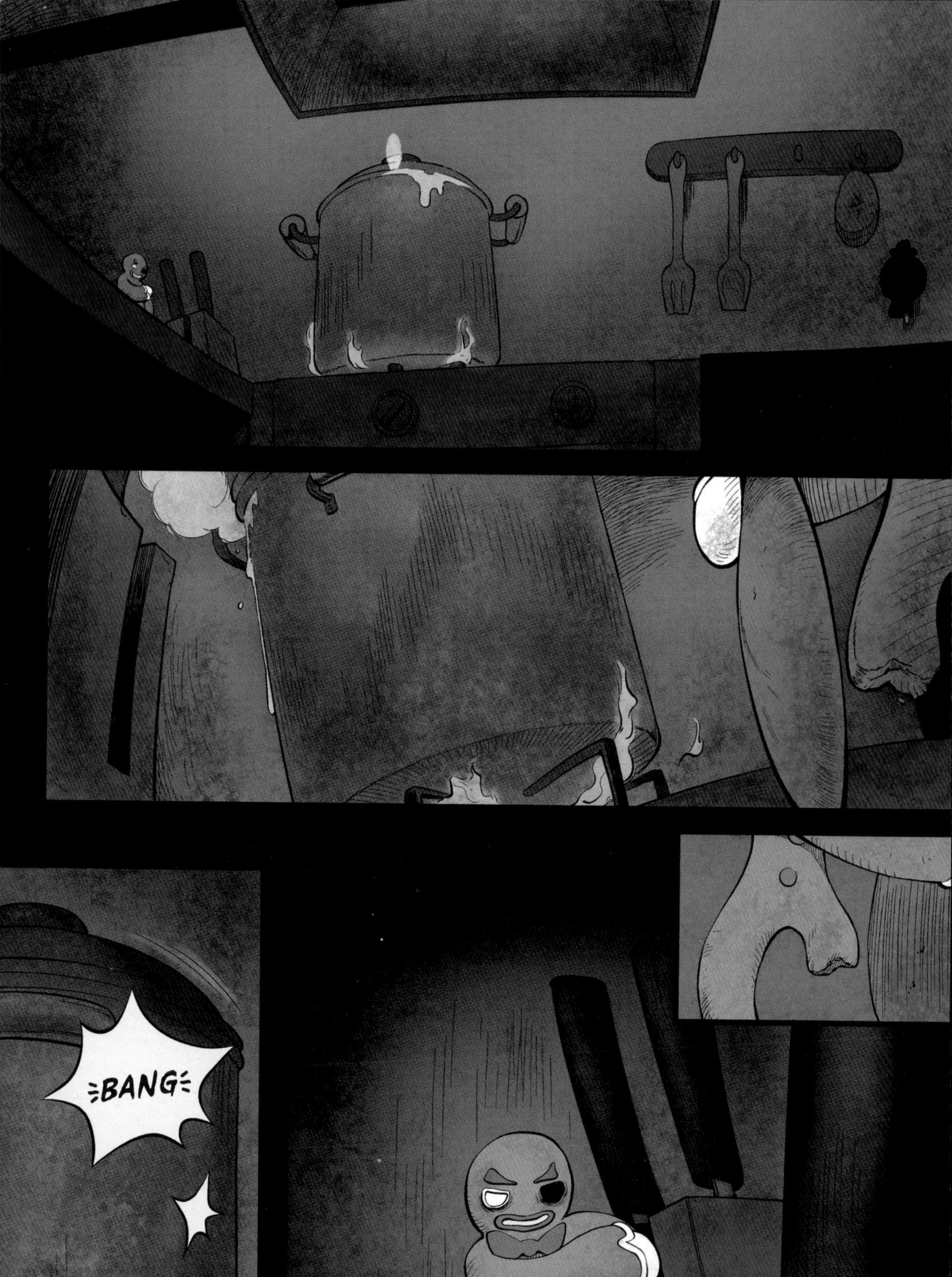

BANG
BANG

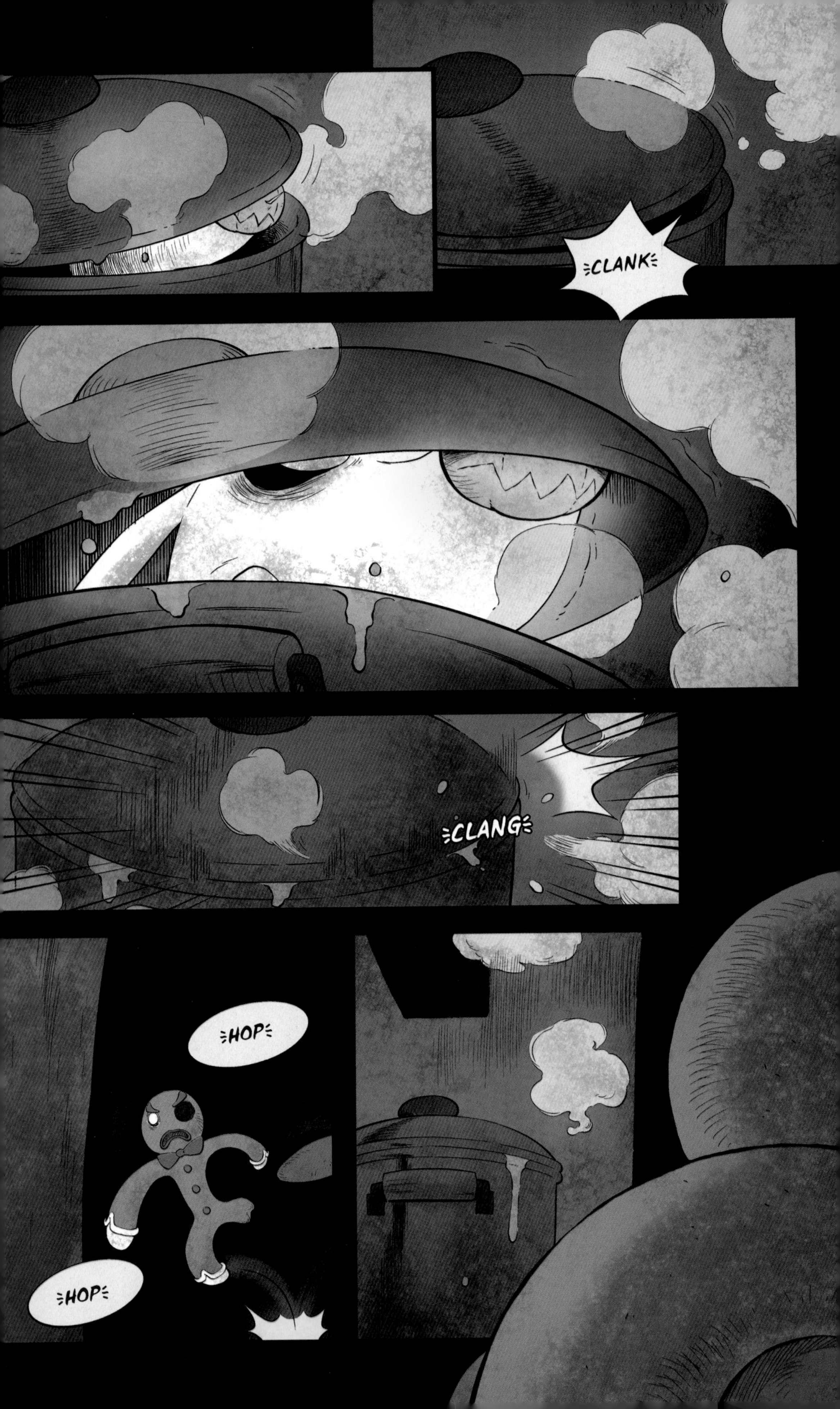
CLANK
CLANG
HOP
HOP

CLANK
CLANK
CLANK
PANT
PANT

SLAM

CHRISTMAS THIS,
CHRISTMAS THAT!
UGH!
I HATE THIS TIME OF YEAR!
...
CLANK
STEP
STEP
CLANG
CREAK
SLAM

CREAK
OH!

WHO IS THIS DOG?!
SLAM

EVERY YEAR ...
...THE MELANCHOLY...
THE HEARTACHE, THE MISERY... WHY AM I STUCK INTHIS DREADFUL TOWN?
THEIR JOYOUS VOICES ALWAYS BRING ME DOWN.
AND YOU!

STOP!
RUINING MY ONLY PLACE OF SOLACE—
-- FOR DESTROYING MY PEACE YOU WILL SUFFER!
I'LL TAKE OUT ALL MY RAGE, IT'S TRUE!
WAIT UNTIL YOU SEE THE THINGS I'LL DO!

BUT SOMEHOW YOU REMIND ME OF ANOTHER...

LICK
TAP
TAP

PEEK
SNAP
SNAP
YOU!
HOW DARE YOU HURT MY BELOVED GINGERBREAD MAN!
CLANK

TREMBLE
YELP!
YELP!
IT'S YOU! MAKING BOISTEROUS NOISE!
I WILL SHOW YOU WHAT IT'S LIKE TO BE ANNOYED!

EVERY YEAR THIS STUPID HOLIDAY—
ALL THE SHOPS CLOSED, SUCH A DELAY--
CLOSED FOR CHRISTMAS
I JUST WISH CHRISTMAS WOULD FINALLY GO AWAY!

OOOH!
THIS STUPID WHITE POWDER FROM THE SKY...
SO COLD AND ICY...
I'M STUCK HERE... WHY OH WHY!
WHINE

GASP
AAOOOOH!
BOO-HOO! MY EARS WILL SPLIT FROM YOUR HORRID SOUND!
IT'S TIME I MAKE SURE YOU'RE NOT AROUND!
I'M THROUGH! WASTING MY PRECIOUS ENERGY AND TIME!

I'LL MAKE YOU PAY FOR YOUR VICIOUS CRIME!
BARK BARK

HAPPY
EASTER ...
NEW YEAR'S DAY
...AND NEW YEAR'S EVE--
-- MAKE ME SCREAM!
THE ONLY HOLIDAY FOR ME IS HALLOWEEN...

BARK
BARK
YOU...
... BETTER THANK YOUR LUCKY STAR--
SLAM
CLANG
--THAT YOU'RE STILL ALIVE AND NOT STEWING IN MY JAR!

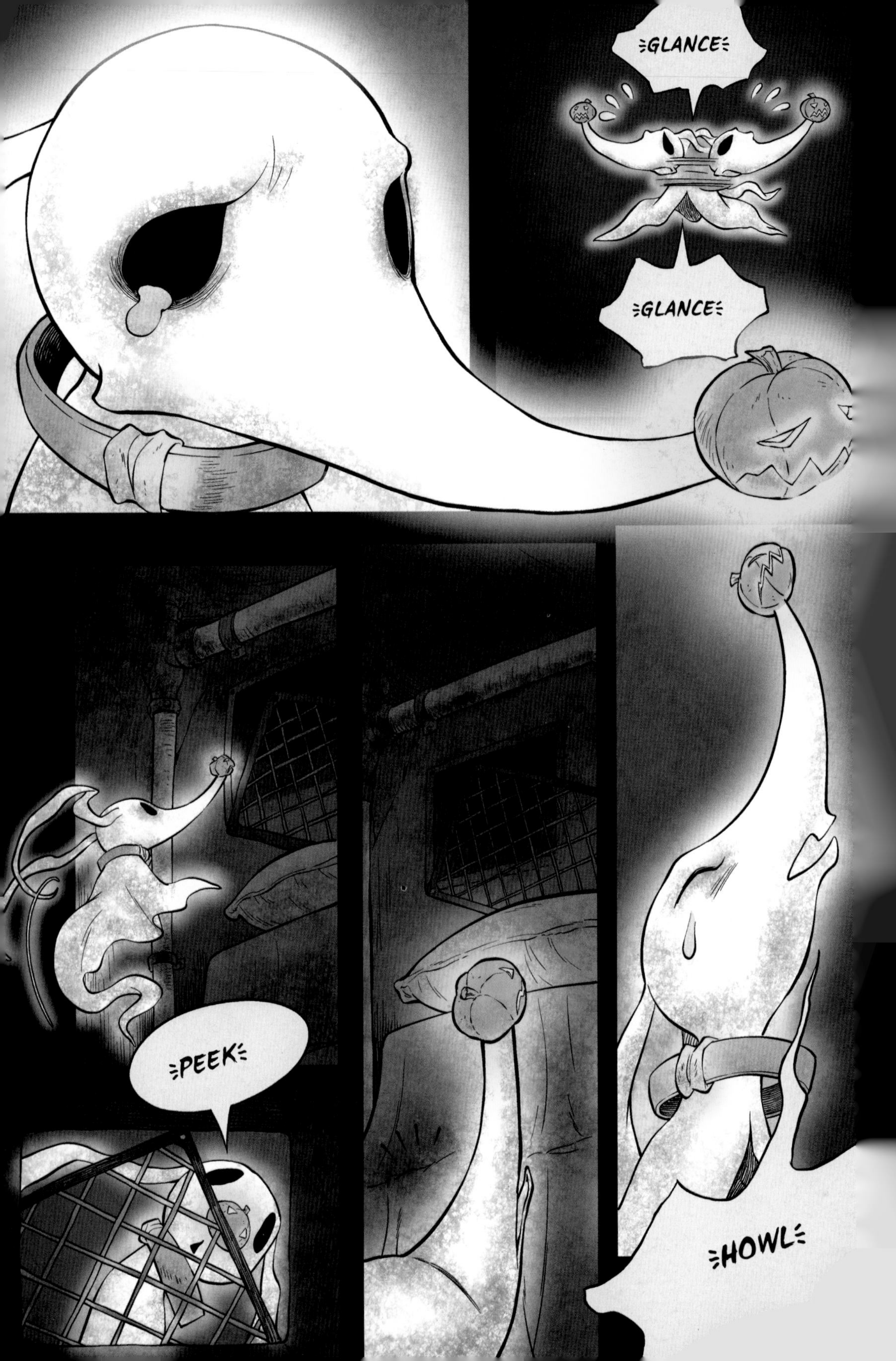
GLANCE
GLANCE
PEEK
HOWL

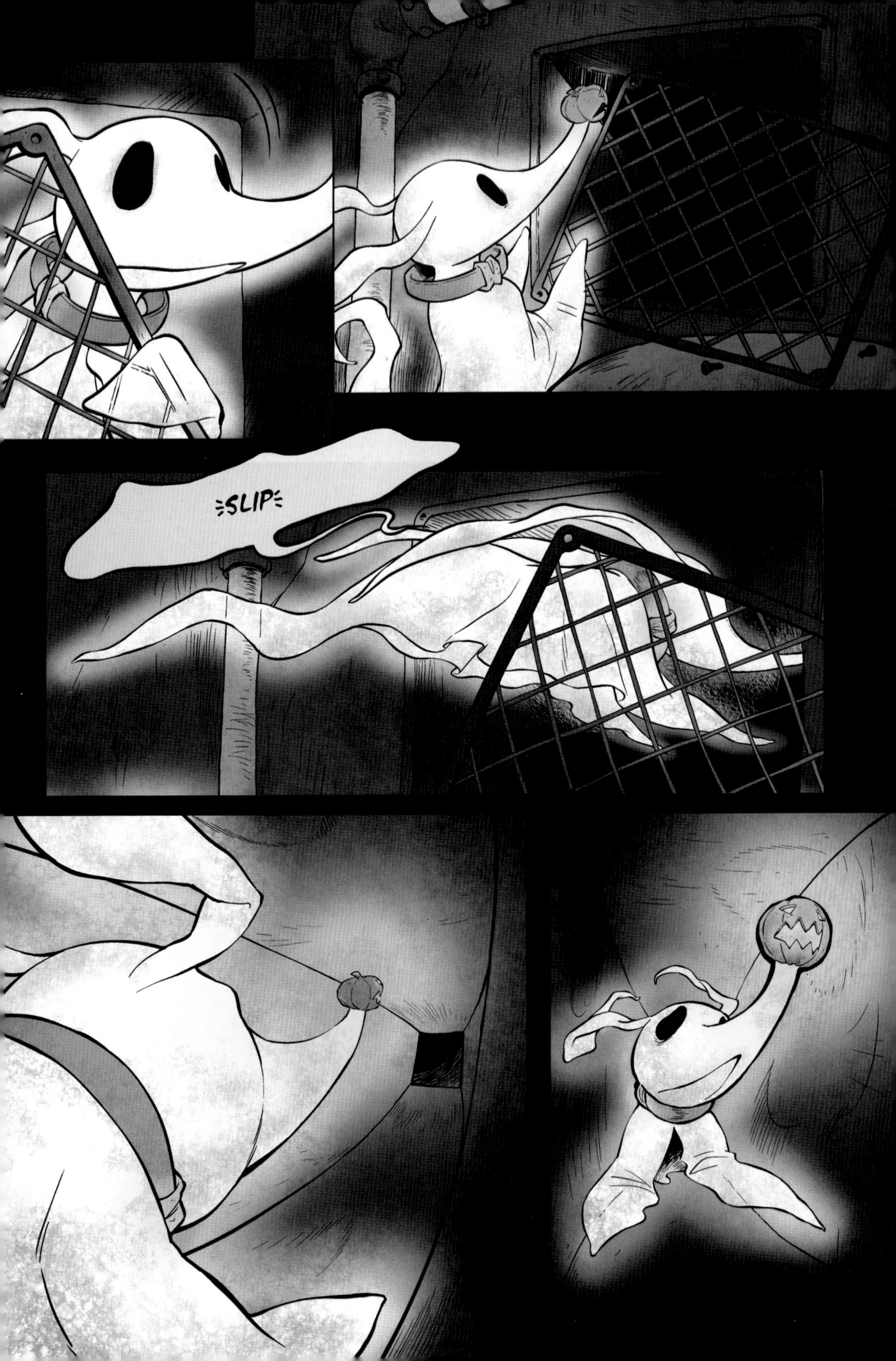
SLIP

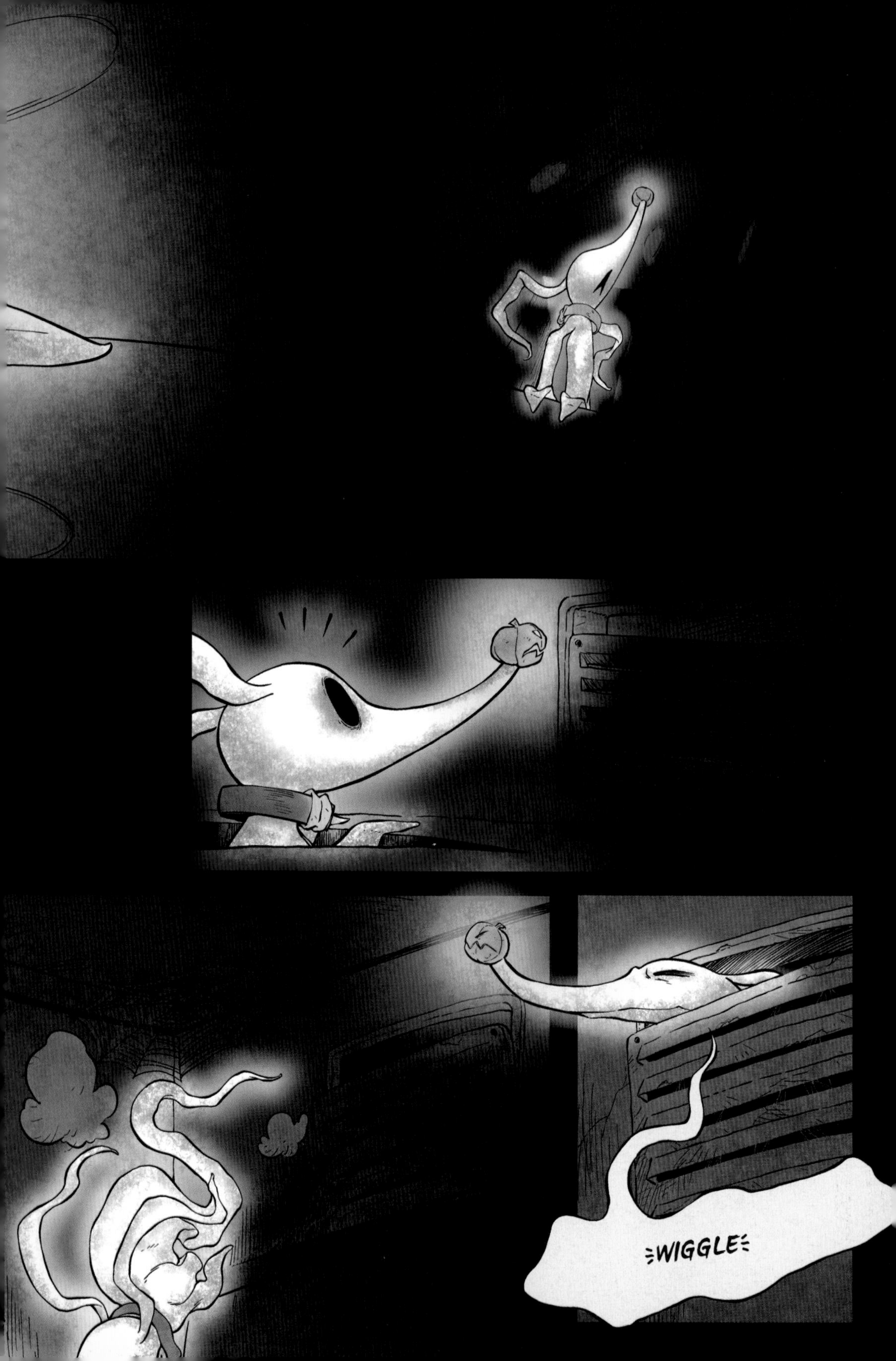
WIGGLE

COUGH
COUG

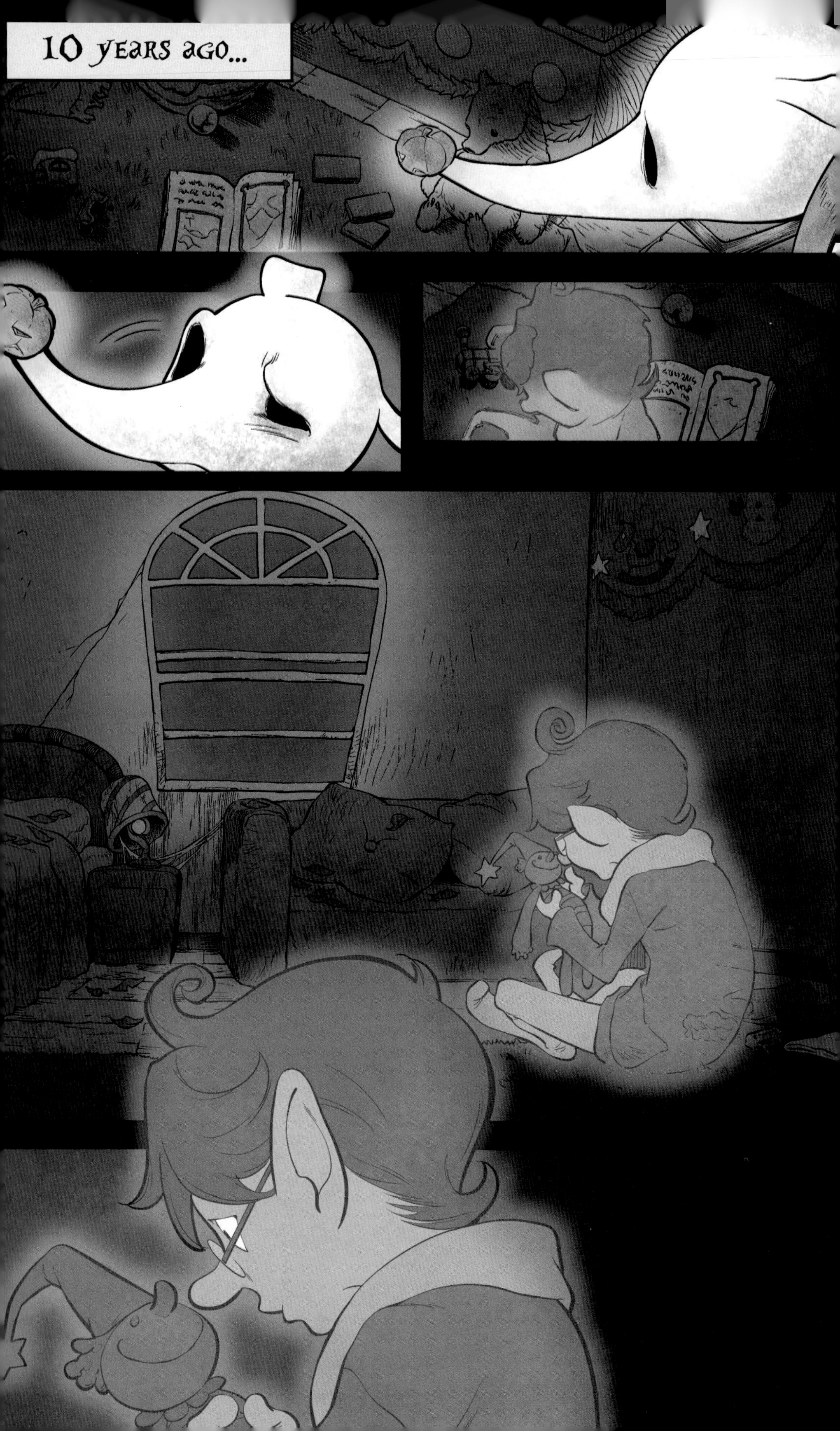
10 years ago...

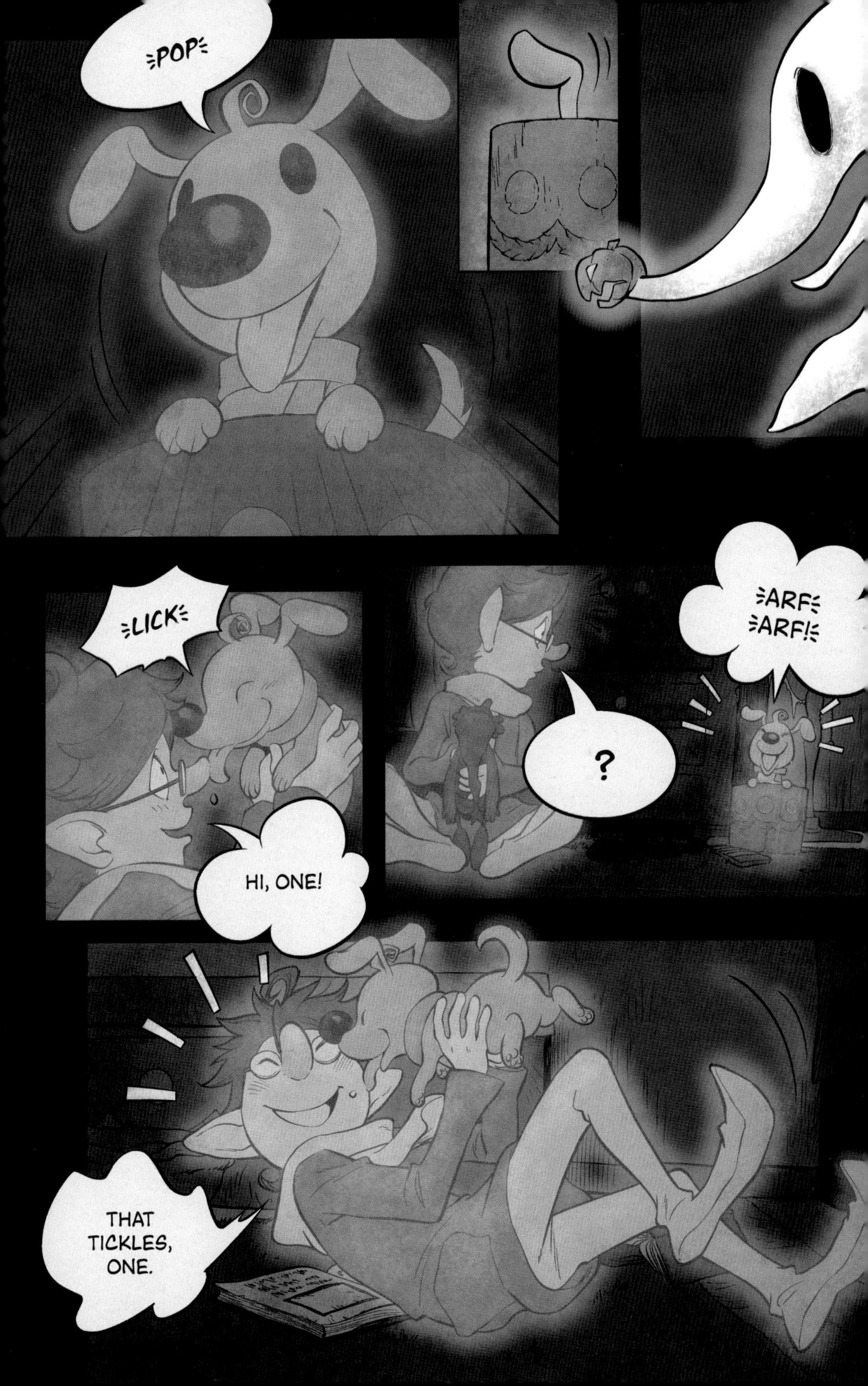
POP
LICK
HI, ONE!
?
ARF ARF!
THAT TICKLES, ONE.

BARK
BARK!
RUSTLE
?
♥

BITE
GOOD BOY.
BRING IT HERE, BOY!
♪

HOW 'BOUT THE BALL?
ARF ARF
BARK BARK

FETCH!
ARF
ARF
CATCH

BITE
BITE
STEP

TRIP

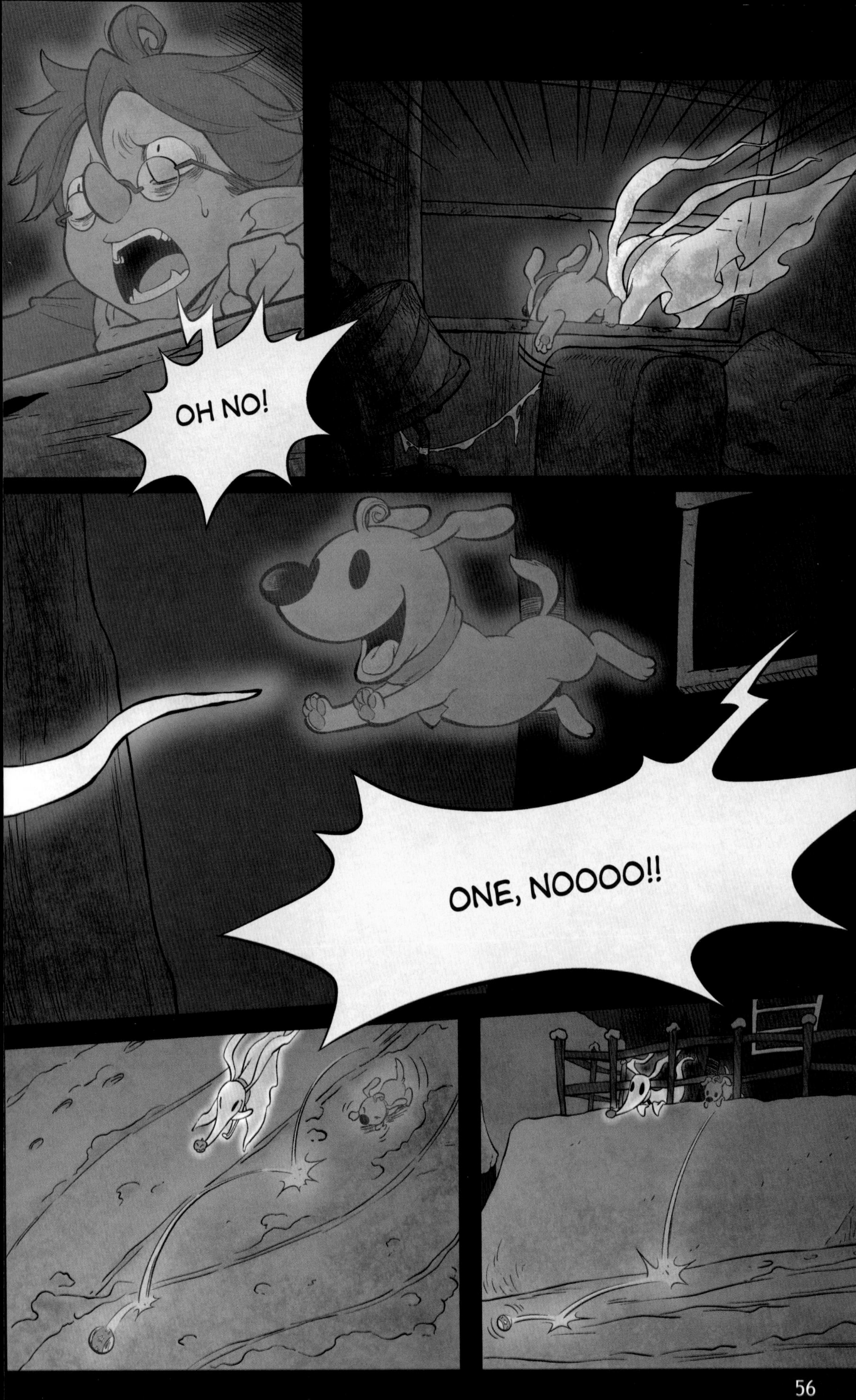
OH NO!
ONE, NOOOO!!

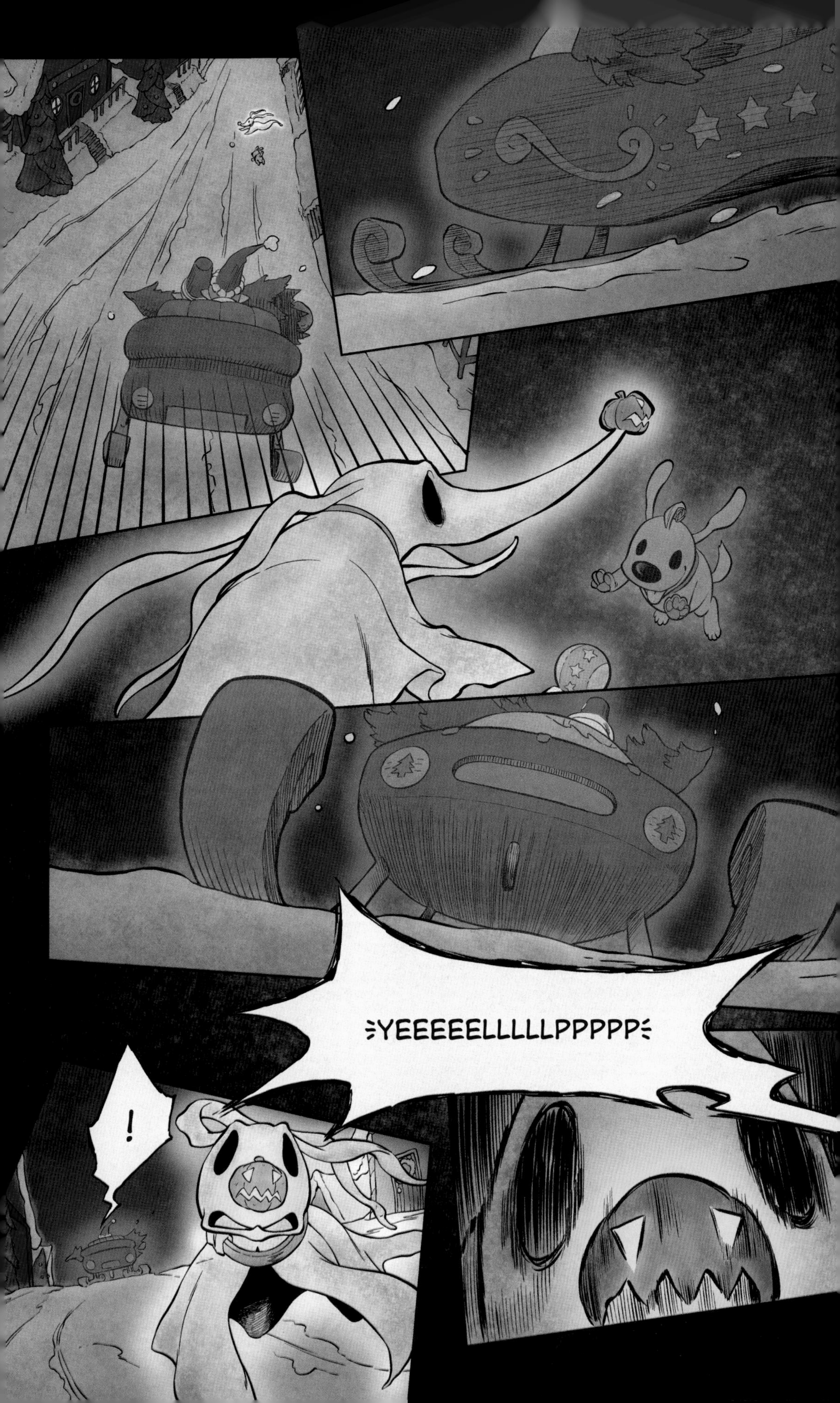
YEEEEELLLLLPPPPP
!

ONE!

YOU POOR THING!
NO!
ONE!
SLIP
I'M SO SORRY, I DIDN'T SEE HIM.
PLEASE FORGIVE US.

FLICKER
FLICKER

ONE...
NO!
I CAN'T BELIEVE THIS HAPPENED.
I'M GOING TO...
...MISS YOU FOREVER!

THIS IS THE WORST DAY EVER!
ARGGH!!
STOMP!
SHOCK
I HATE CHRISTMAS!
GLIDE

WOBBLE
SLAM

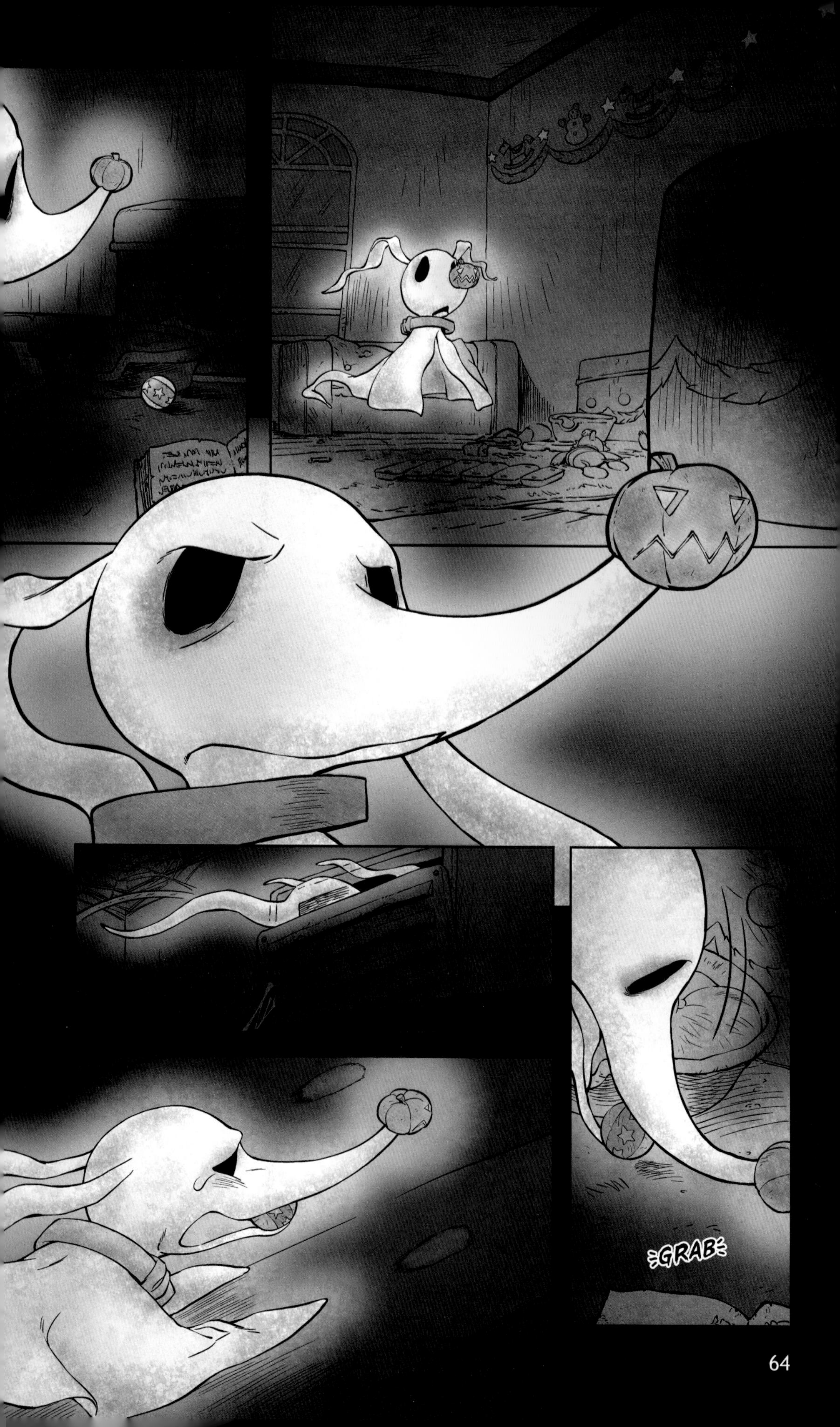
GRAB

WHERE ARE THOSE TWO?!
HEY...
CRUNCH
CRUNCH

WHAT HAPPENED TO YOU?
NO, WHAT HAPPENED TO YOU? WHAT'S THAT WHITE STUFF ALL OVER YOU?

WHAT...?
WH...
NOTHING.
LOOKS LIKE SOMEONE HAD FUN!
AHAHAHAHAHHA!!
WHAT HAPPENED TO YOU?!

SMEAR
RUB
THE PAIN... IT HURTS!
AHAHA!
I'M THE ONE WHO CRASHED--
IT'S ME WHO HURTS!

TOO...MUCH...
...
WHAT'S WRONG WITH YOU?
YOU PIG!
...CANDY!!
LOOK WHO'S TALKING!
GREEDY GUTS!

KNOCK IT OFF,
YOU IDIOTS!
HAHAHAHAHA!
WE'VE GOT TO
FIND ZERO!

I HAVE AN IDEA.
MY HUNCH IS HE'S WITH THE TOYS.
YEAH, IN THE TOY STORE!
YOU KNOW, WE NEED TO GO LOOK FOR HIM...
HUH?

CRUNCH
CRUNCH

SLIDE
DRAG
?

RUN!

HEY!

SCAMPER
ZIP
DASH
SLAM

THIEVES!
CATCH THEM!
THEY STOLE FROM ME!

YOU THIEVES!
GET BACK HERE!
BOING

GRAB
CHAOS, CHAOS, CHAOS IN CHRISTMAS TOWN TONIGHT!
LOCK, SHOCK AND BARREL WREAKING HAVOC EVERYWHERE IN SIGHT!

CHAOS, CHAOS, CHAOS IN CHRISTMAS TOWN TODAY!
'TIL WE GET OUR FILL OF ANARCHY...
...IN CHRISTMAS TOWN WE'LL STAY!
HOOOORAY!!

DASH
SPLIT UP!
I'M OPEN!
KICK IT HERE!
SQUEEEEZE
OOF!
WHOMP

HAHA, LOOK AT HIM!
OOGLE
WEIRDO!
SCAMPER

SEE YOU AGA
SCURRY

CHRISTMAS MARKET

CRASH
FLEE
BONK
!
!
SHATTER
HEY, LOOK WHAT YOU'VE DONE!
FLEE

WHEW, THAT WAS ROUGH!
I'M EXHAUSTED!
PANT
PANT
JUST GETTING OUT OF BED EXHAUSTS YOU!
GET THEM!!
THERE!

SLIP

TAP
ROLL
DROP

TUG
TUG
TUG
TUG

POKE
POKE
!

BARK!
BARK!
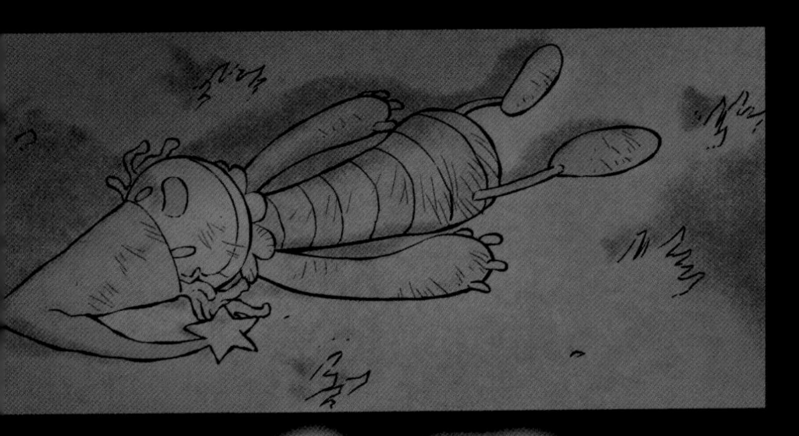
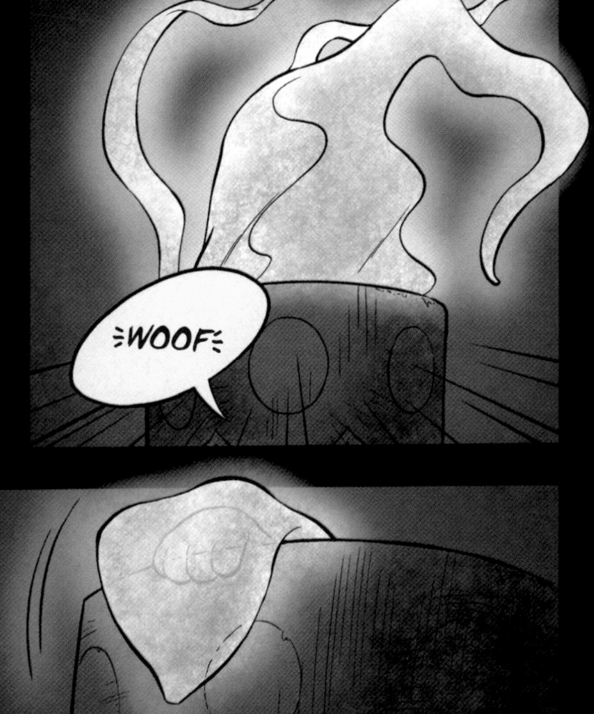
WOOF

SNIFF
SNIFF

WOOF
POP

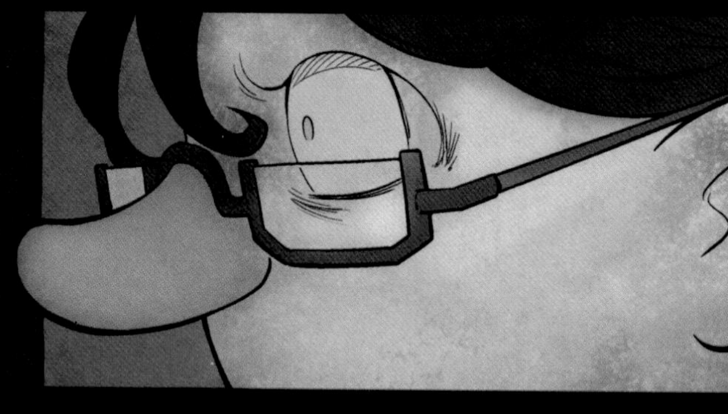
IT CAN'T BE TRUE...

...ONE?

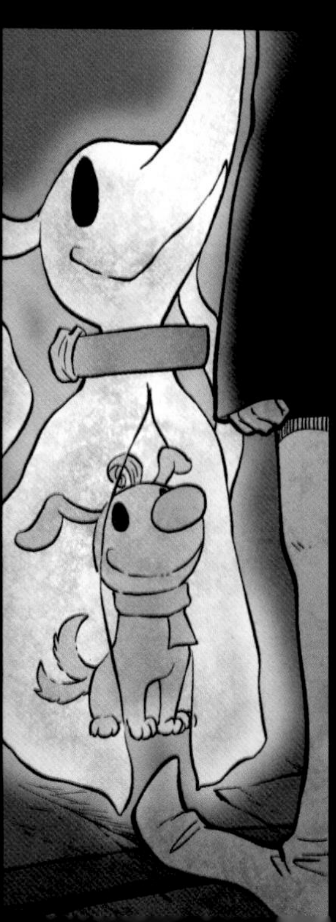

ARF!
ONE -- MY LITTLE PUPPY! IS THIS REALLY YOU?!
LICK

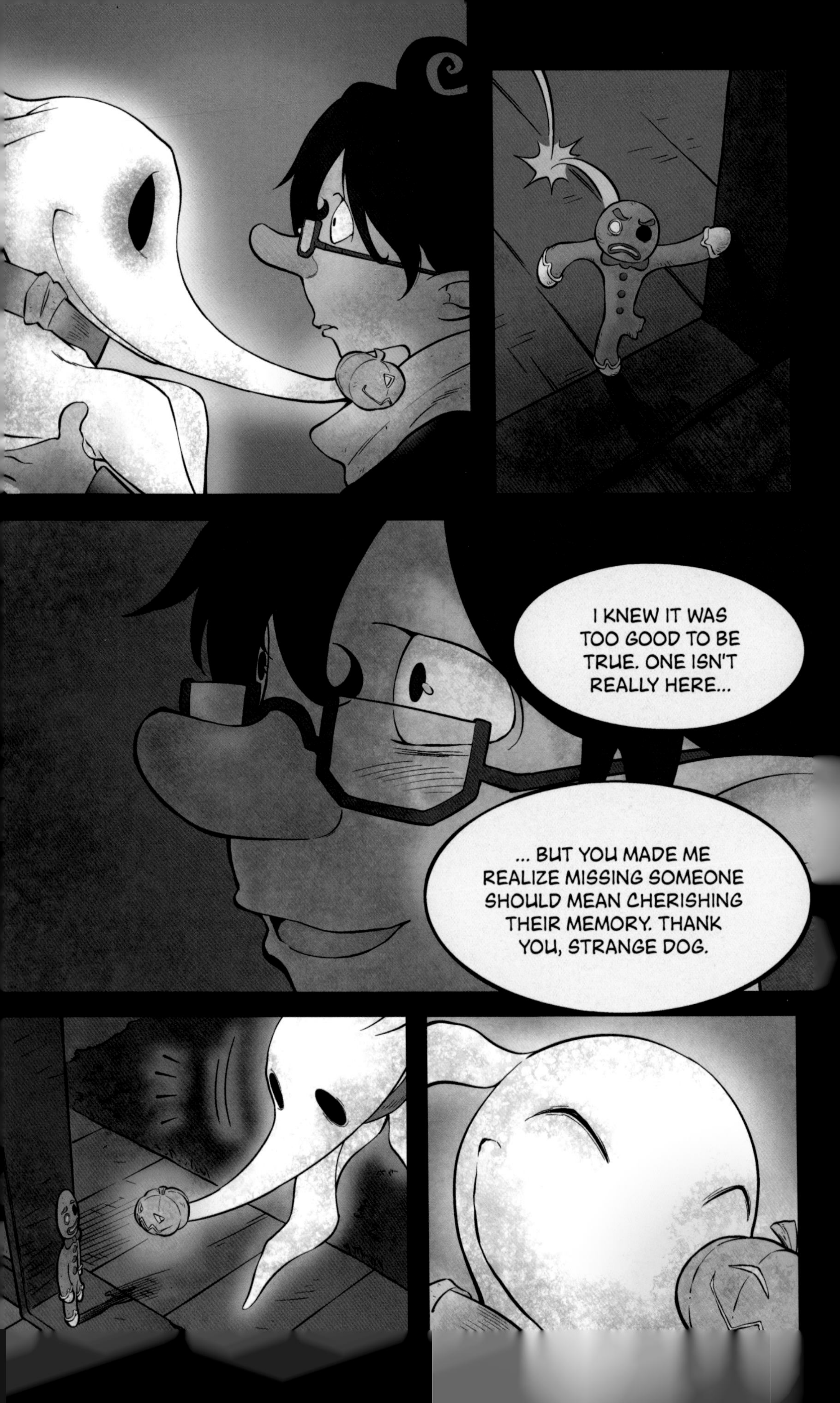
I KNEW IT WAS
TOO GOOD TO BE
TRUE. ONE ISN'T
REALLY HERE...
... BUT YOU MADE ME
REALIZE MISSING SOMEONE
SHOULD MEAN CHERISHING
THEIR MEMORY. THANK
YOU, STRANGE DOG.

GRAB
KA-CHK!
CREEEK

I'M SORRY FOR BEING SO CRUEL, HALLOWEEN DOG.
MISTER MYZER AND I WISH YOU A MERRY CHRISTMAS!
SLIP

HOLIDAY DOORS
SNIFF
SNIFF

STOP!
HEY!

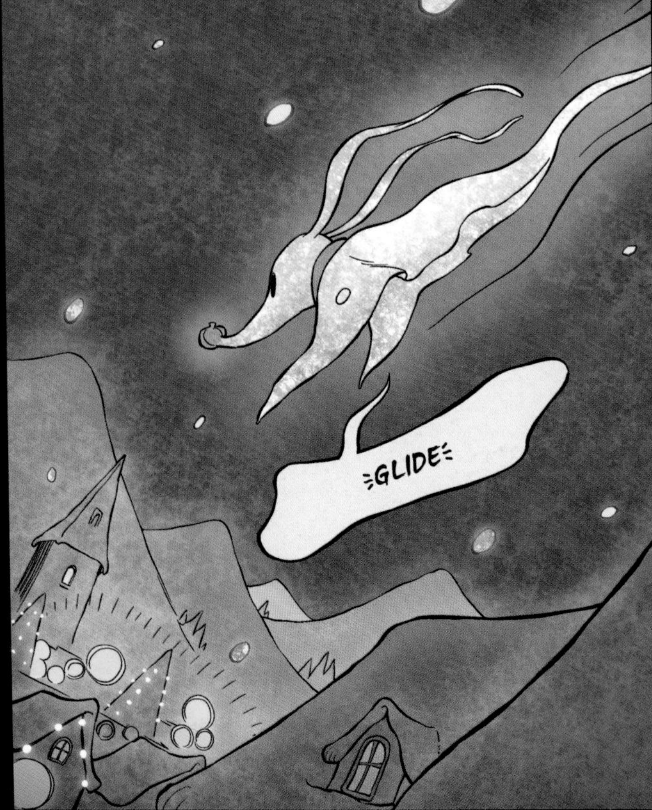
GLIDE

HEY!
HALT!
GET THEM!!
GET BACK HERE!
AH!
CRASH

SKID
OUCH
ZERO!
ZERO!
WE FOUND YOU!!

ZERO!
THERE THEY ARE!!
GET THEM!!
UH-OH...

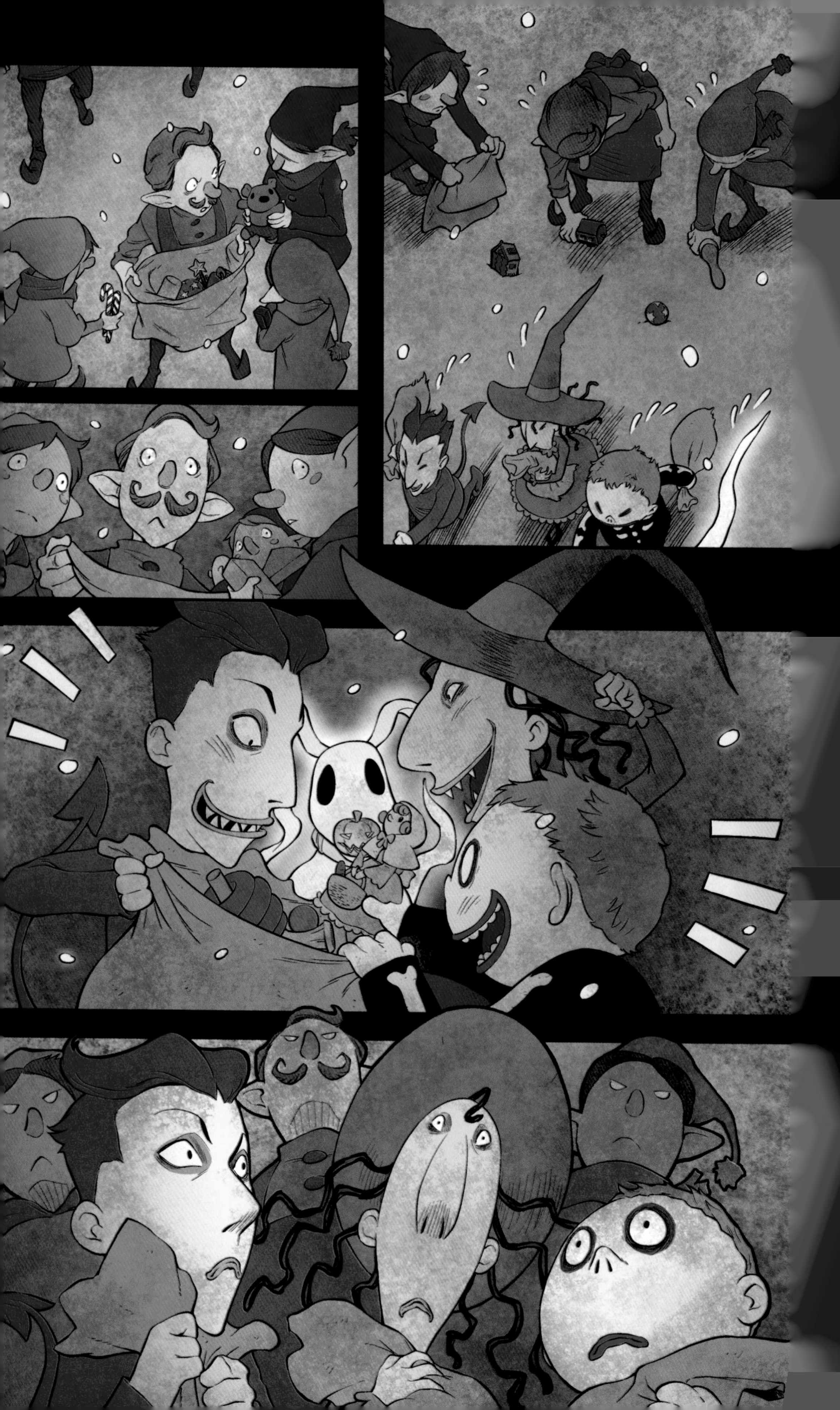

OWW!

RUN AWAY!

HURRY!

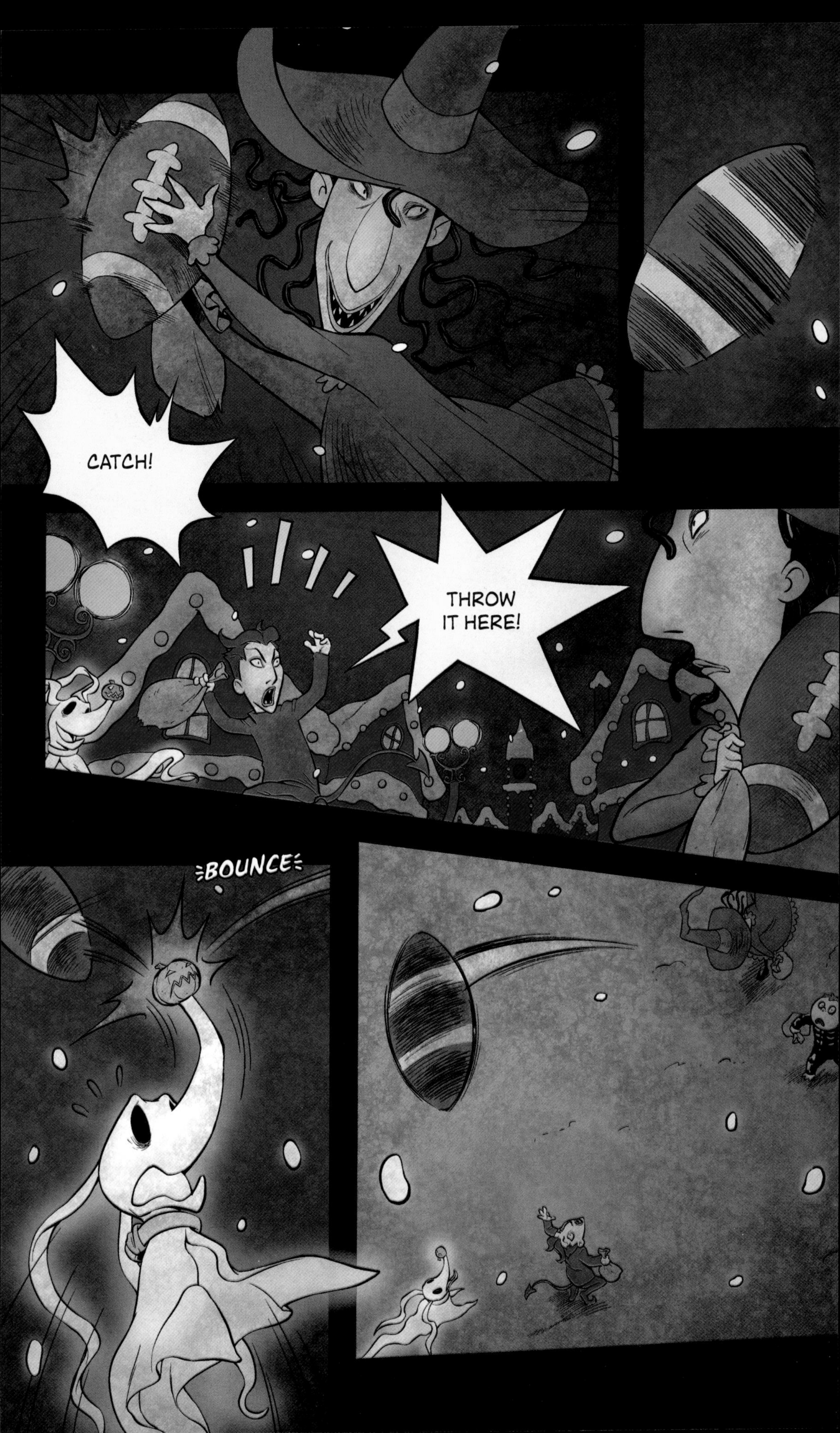
CATCH!
THROW IT HERE!
BOUNCE

SPLURT

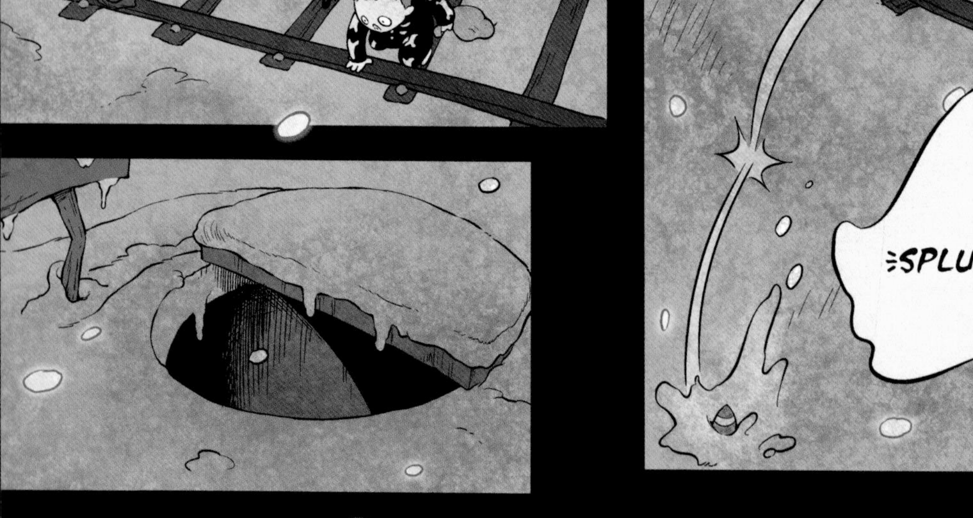

CAUTION

SLIP

AH!
AH!
AH!
AGH!
AGH!
DIVE
TO BE CONTINUED

COMING SOON

Zero's on an important quest!

Going home will have to wait just a little longer...

Follow the release schedule and find out what happens next at
TOKYOPOP.com/upcoming!

Zero's Journey

COVER GALLERY

ISSUE #5

MAIN COVER (KIYOSHI ARAI)

ISSUE #6

MAIN COVER (KIYOSHI ARAI)

ISSUE #7

MAIN COVER (KIYOSHI ARAI)

ISSUE #8

MAIN COVER (KIYOSHI ARAI)

ISSUE #9

MAIN COVER (KIYOSHI ARAI)

GRAPHIC NOVEL #2

FINAL COVER (KIYOSHI ARAI)

GRAPHIC NOVEL #2

COVER SKETCH (KIYOSHI ARAI)

COVER CREATION - BEHIND THE SCENES

ISSUE #5 COVER SKETCH 1

ISSUE #5 COVER SKETCH 2

ISSUE #7 COVER SKETCH

ISSUE #6 COVER SKETCH

COVER CREATION - BEHIND THE SCENES

ISSUE #8 COVER SKETCH 1

ISSUE #8 COVER SKETCH 2

ISSUE #9 COVER SKETCH

Disney

Tim Burton's The Nightmare Before Christmas

Zero's Journey

CONCEPT GALLERY

MISTER MYZER

ORIGINAL CONCEPT (KIYOSHI ARAI)

GINGERBREAD MAN

CONCEPT (KIYOSHI ARAI)

MIDDLE-AGED COUPLE

CONCEPT (KIYOSHI ARAI)

Middle-aged couple
in Christmas Town

Kiyoshi Arai
18.09.20

Middle-aged couple
in Christmas Town

Kiyoshi Arai
18.09.20

PROPS

CONCEPT (JUN SUZUKI)

CHRISTMAS TOWN SLED

CHRISTMAS TOWN SLED

CHRISTMAS TOWN SLED

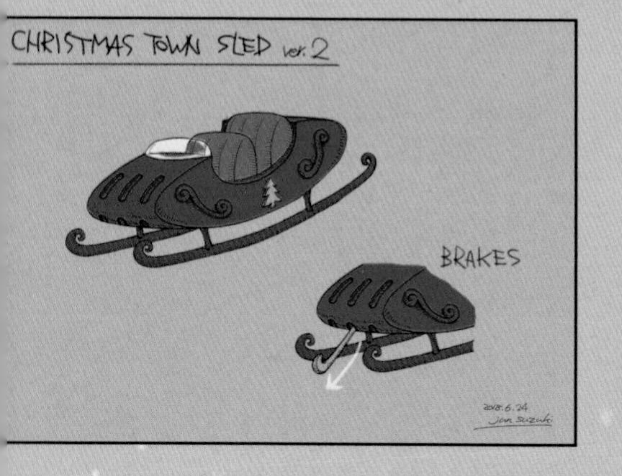

CHRISTMAS TOWN SLED

CHRISTMAS TOWN SLED

PROPS

CONCEPT (JUN SUZUKI)

NEW YEAR'S ARCH

NEW YEAR'S ARCH

CHRISTMAS TOWN SIGNS

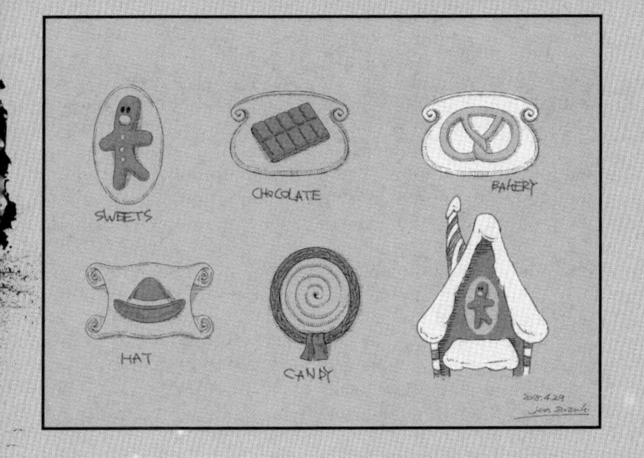

MR. MYZER'S KAMADO (COOK STOVE)

LOCATIONS

CONCEPTS (KIYOSHI ARAI AND JUN SUZUKI)

MR. MYZER'S HOUSE - ROUGH DESIGNS

LOCATIONS

CONCEPTS (KIYOSHI ARAI AND JUN SUZUKI)

RESIDENTIAL AREA (JUN SUZUKI)